This
MOUSE ⬡ WORKS
Classics Collection Storybook

belongs to

_____

DISNEY's

THE
LION KING II
SIMBA'S · PRIDE
CLASSIC STORYBOOK

*Find us at **www.disneybooks.com*** *for more Mouse Works fun!*

© 1998 Disney Enterprises, Inc.
Adapted by Victoria Saxon
Illustrated by John and Andrea Alvin
Printed in the United States of America
ISBN: 1-57082-876-8
1 3 5 7 9 10 8 6 4 2

As the winds swirled majestically around Pride Rock, Simba and Nala nuzzled each other. Rafiki the baboon was presenting their new cub to all the animals of the Pride Lands.

"Look at the little guy," Timon gushed. "A chip off the old block."

Just then, Rafiki made an announcement: "It is a girl!"

Simba and Nala beamed with pride.

"A GIRL?" yelled Timon. "Oy!"

Later that evening, Rafiki stood in his tree, happily painting a picture of Simba's newborn daughter, Kiara.

"Oh, Mufasa," Rafiki said to the spirit of Simba's father, "another circle of life is complete!"

But in response, Mufasa made a wind blow. He was warning Rafiki that there was trouble brewing nearby.

The trouble lay in the Outlands, where the evil lioness Zira was plotting to avenge the death of Simba's uncle Scar. Long ago, Simba had banished Scar's followers to the Outlands.

Before his death, Scar had named Zira's son Kovu as his heir. Now Zira was training Kovu to overthrow Simba and take his place as king.

Just then Kovu's brother and sister, Nuka and Vitani, returned from a secret trip to the Pride Lands.

"Simba's new cub is a girl!" Vitani reported eagerly.

Zira smiled. "Only boys," she growled, "will be kings."

"Yeah," said Nuka. "Maybe I should be the leader."

"Don't be a fool, Nuka!" Zira cried. Under Zira's plan, everyone had a role to play. Kovu would become king. Nuka and Vitani were merely in charge of protecting him.

Several months later, Kiara was prancing and dancing on Pride Rock, ready to go out and play.

"Now remember," Simba lectured to his cub, "stay in sight of Pride Rock at all times. And stay away from the Outlands."

Kiara promised to be careful as she raced away. Then Simba turned to Timon and Pumbaa. He asked them to follow her and make sure she was safe.

Kiara wasn't expecting to have two baby sitters on her trail, so when she accidentally stumbled upon Timon and Pumbaa she was startled—and a bit angry.

When Timon and Pumbaa started arguing over their lunch, Kiara saw her opportunity to escape. She quietly slipped away.

Enjoying her freedom, Kiara scampered happily down a steep incline toward a swampy river. There she came face to face with a strange cub from the Outlands!

Fleeing the stranger, Kiara ran across some rocks in the swamp. Suddenly one of the rocks moved. Kiara realized she was standing on a crocodile!

The other cub scrambled and jumped across the backs of the crocodiles, racing desperately to reach the shore as huge jaws snapped all around them.

As soon as the two cubs safely reached the shore, Kiara began chattering excitedly about their adventure.

"My name's Kiara," she said. "You were really brave."

"I'm Kovu," the other cub said hesitantly. "You were pretty brave, too." Neither cub knew that Zira was spying on them.

Quickly Kiara ran up to Kovu and tagged him. "You're it!" she shouted happily. But Kovu just looked puzzled.

"Don't you know how to play?" Kiara asked.

Just then, Simba appeared! He had been looking all over the Pride Lands for Kiara. When he saw Kovu with her, Simba leaped to protect his daughter.

But as he did, Zira emerged from her hiding place in the bushes and faced him. "Simba," she hissed evilly.

Zira was just about to attack Simba, when she heard a growl from behind him. It was Nala. And behind her were Timon and Pumbaa. If Zira fought, she would be badly outnumbered.

Instead, Zira coyly introduced Kovu as Scar's chosen heir—and the next leader of the Pride Lands. Simba understood the threat.

"Take your cub and get out," Simba said. "We're through here."

"Oh, no," Zira replied slyly. "We've barely begun." Then she picked up Kovu and started back toward the Outlands.

Simba picked up Kiara and headed toward the Pride Lands.

The two cubs quietly bid each other good-bye. They would miss playing together.

"Kiara," Simba said when they were alone together, "you need to be careful. You're going to be a queen someday."

Kiara looked enviously at a bird flying freely from its nest. She was not sure that she wanted to be a queen.

"It's part of who you are," Simba replied. "All the animals around you, your family—we are one. We are all part of the circle of life."

In the Outlands, Vitani was sharpening her teeth on a dried-up root. She was surprised to see Nuka approach. "Where's Kovu?" she asked.

"Hey, it's every lion for himself out there," Nuka replied carelessly.

"Mother's gonna be mad," Vitani warned. "She told you to watch him."

Moments later, Zira returned with Kovu. Nuka and Vitani raced to greet them, but Zira lashed out at Nuka.

"It was my fault, Mother," Kovu interrupted. "I wandered off on my own. When I met Kiara, I thought we could be friends—"

"Friends!" Zira hissed sarcastically. Then she stopped. She realized Kovu had a good idea.

Zira carried Kovu over to his bed while all the other Outsiders watched. She now knew that the way to overthrow Simba was through his daughter. She would groom Kovu to get close to Kiara. When he did, Kovu would be able to get rid of Simba and take over the Pride Lands for good.

Seasons passed. Kiara and Kovu grew into young adults.

One day Rafiki stood in his tree drawing a picture of Kovu next to Kiara. He was worried about the growing tension between the Outsiders and the Pride Landers.

"Kiara and Kovu together? This is the plan?" Rafiki asked aloud. He had heard Mufasa's voice in the wind.

In the Outlands, Kovu stood staunchly in front of the Outsiders while Zira inspected him.

"You are ready," Zira pronounced. The other Outsiders roared their approval.

At the same time, on Pride Rock, Timon and Pumbaa were sobbing tears of joy. It was the day of Kiara's first solo hunt.

"Daddy," Kiara said as she started out toward the plains, "promise that you'll let me do this on my own."

With Nala standing by his side, Simba smiled weakly. "All right," he said. "I promise."

But soon Simba realized he couldn't stand the possibility of Kiara's being in any kind of danger. He had to break his promise. Quietly, he asked Timon and Pumbaa to go after his daughter.

Timon and Pumbaa took their mission seriously. They had to protect Kiara without letting her know they were nearby. They ducked under rocks, scooted behind trees, and belly-crawled through tall grasses. Then they came face to face with...Kiara!

Kiara felt betrayed. Simba had promised to let her hunt on her own! She raced away from Timon and Pumbaa as fast as she could.

Meanwhile, Zira had put her master plan in motion. She sent Nuka and Vitani to start a fire near Kiara in the Pride Lands.

When Kiara finally noticed the fire closing in on her, she raced to escape, but soon was overcome by smoke. Just when it looked as if Kiara might be lost forever, Kovu appeared. Braving the smoke and flames, Kovu dragged Kiara to a nearby swamp.

When Kiara regained consciousness, she was furious.

"Why did you bring me here?" she asked the strange lion who had rescued her. "Who do you think you are?"

As she spoke, Kiara leaped to her feet, but Kovu splashed into the water, blocking her way. Kiara hesitated. There was something familiar about this lion.

"Kovu?" she asked, finally recognizing her rescuer.

Just then, Simba and Nala arrived with Rafiki. They had seen the fire from Pride Rock.

"I humbly ask to join your pride," Kovu said to Simba.

Simba hesitated. Kovu was an Outsider, but he had just saved Kiara's life.

Reluctantly, Simba decided to allow Kovu to return to
Pride Rock with his family.

However, he still did not trust Kovu. That night, Simba
would not let Kovu inside his cave with the rest of the pride.

Not far from Pride Rock, Nuka and Zira sat perched on a tree limb, watching Kovu's every move.

When Kiara came out of the cave to speak with Kovu, Nuka perked up. He wanted to see Kovu get rid of Kiara and her father once and for all. But Kovu merely spoke with Kiara until she returned to the cave.

That night, Simba had a horrible nightmare. He dreamed about Scar betraying Mufasa, but saw Kovu in his dream, instead of Scar. Simba awoke in a fright, wondering again whether he should trust the young lion who was sleeping outside his cave.

Simba had reason to worry. Kovu had been trained his whole life to believe Simba was his enemy. The next morning, when Simba was making his rounds of the Pride Lands, Kovu watched him and readied himself to attack. But something made him hesitate.

"Good morning!" came a voice behind him. It was Kiara.

The two lions set out into the plains together. Kovu had promised Kiara that he would teach her how to stalk. But when Kiara tried to pounce on Kovu, he merely ducked and sent her sprawling.

"Did you hear me sneaking up on you?" Kiara asked.

"Only a lot," Kovu replied with a huge sigh.

As Kiara and Kovu continued across the Pride
Lands, they soon came upon Timon and Pumbaa.
Timon explained that they had been searching for
bugs, but there were too many birds in the way.

"We'll help!" said Kiara as she and Kovu raced
down the hill, roaring. The birds flew away! One
bird even gave Timon a ride.

Kovu followed Kiara across the landscape, chasing birds. He laughed out loud. This was fun!

Suddenly the friends skidded to a halt. They had run right into a herd of rhinoceros.

Quickly, they turned around and raced in the opposite direction—away from a stampede!

"A-a-ah!" cried Pumbaa.

Finally the friends found shelter in a small cave. Kovu and Kiara giggled in relief with Timon and Pumbaa.

"You're okay, kid," Timon said to Kovu.

Kovu smiled. As he squirmed to get out of the cave, he realized how close he was to Kiara, and how much he enjoyed being with her.

Later that night Kiara and Kovu lay on their backs and looked up at the vast expanse of sky above them.

"My father and I used to do this all the time," Kiara said. "He says all the great kings of the past are up there."

Kovu had been brought up to believe that the Pride Landers were his enemies. He now was beginning to doubt everything Zira had taught him.

On a nearby hill, Simba was also having doubts. "Father," he said, looking up at the stars, "I am lost. Kovu is Scar's heir. How can I trust him?"

But Simba heard no answers from his father that night. Instead Nala approached. She gently urged him to get to know Kovu better. Perhaps Kovu would choose to follow a different path than the one Zira and Scar had chosen for him.

Meanwhile, Rafiki was doing his part to help Kovu make the decision to stay a Pride Lander.

"Follow me," Rafiki said to Kiara and Kovu. "We are going to a special place in your heart. It is called Upendi." Rafiki smiled happily. Kiara and Kovu were falling in love!

When Kovu returned to Pride Rock with Kiara, Simba finally invited him to join the rest of the pride inside his cave.

From a safe distance, Vitani watched Kovu. Then she ran back to the Outlands to report to Zira.

"No!" Zira replied angrily. "Kovu is betraying us!"

"I think I know how we can stop him," Nuka said slyly.

The next morning, Simba and Kovu went for a walk together. Simba explained how Scar had been unable to let go of the hatred in his heart, and how it had eventually destroyed him.

Though disappointed about Scar, Kovu knew that Simba was right.

Just then, Simba heard a noise. He turned and saw Zira facing him with several other Outsiders. It was an ambush!

Thinking Kovu had helped set up the ambush, Simba struggled to escape the attacking Outsiders. Quickly, he jumped into a ravine. Then, with nowhere else to go, Simba scrambled onto a high pile of logs. The logs were perched on top of one another. A single wrong step would make them fall.

Nuka was the only Outsider foolish enough to advance. When he jumped up, the logs began to tumble, and Simba quickly leaped to safety.

When the logs stopped rolling, Nuka lay beneath the pile. Zira ran a gentle paw over her son as he took his last breath. Then she turned toward Kovu. In her anger, she struck him, creating a slash over his eye exactly like the one Scar once had.

Kovu turned from Zira and headed back toward the Pride Lands. He now knew where his loyalties belonged: with Simba...and with Kiara.

But when Kovu reached Pride Rock, he met the scorn of thousands of animals. All the Pride Landers thought that Kovu had intentionally led Simba into the Outsiders' ambush.

From the top of Pride Rock, Simba pronounced Kovu's fate: exile from the Pride Lands forever. Kiara tried to defend Kovu, but Simba would not back down from his decision.

Alone in the cave at Pride Rock, Kiara made up her mind to follow Kovu into exile. Quickly, she slipped out of the cave and made her way across the Pride Lands toward the places beyond the edge of her father's kingdom.

When Kiara finally found Kovu, he was overjoyed to see her—and to know that someone believed him.

Together they went to drink from a water hole. "Look!" Kovu said, looking at their shared reflection in the water. "We are one."

It was at that moment that Kiara realized they should return to the Pride Lands and bring about a peace between their prides.

As Kiara and Kovu headed home, Zazu raced to find Simba. Zazu had spotted the Outsiders getting ready to attack the Pride Landers.

Simba quickly ordered the pride to prepare for battle.

As the clouds darkened the skies over the plains, the Outsiders and the Pride Landers approached their battleground.

Then the fighting began.

Amid pouring rain and thunder, Kiara and Kovu raced onward. When they came upon the battle, Kiara leaped into its midst to talk to Simba.

"Daddy, this has to stop!" Kiara pleaded. Then she repeated the same words Simba had taught her long ago. "A wise king once told me," she said, "we are one."

Simba hesitated only a moment before calling for peace.

Furious at this turn of events, Zira lunged at Simba. But Kiara jumped to block her attack. Together, the two lionesses rolled over a small cliff at the edge of a deep gorge.

Clinging to the side of the gorge, Kiara reached out to help Zira. But Zira only lashed back at Kiara. A moment later, a dam of logs broke apart, causing a massive wall of water to fill the gorge. Kiara managed to climb to safety, but Zira fell and was lost forever.

Days later, the Pride Landers and Outsiders gathered together in a great circle at Pride Rock. There Rafiki performed a ceremony to celebrate their union.

As Simba gazed proudly at his daughter sitting next to Kovu, he heard a voice in the wind. It was Mufasa.

"Well done, my son," the voice said. "We are one."

Disney's Classic Storybook

COLLECTION ™

Relive the movies one book at a time.

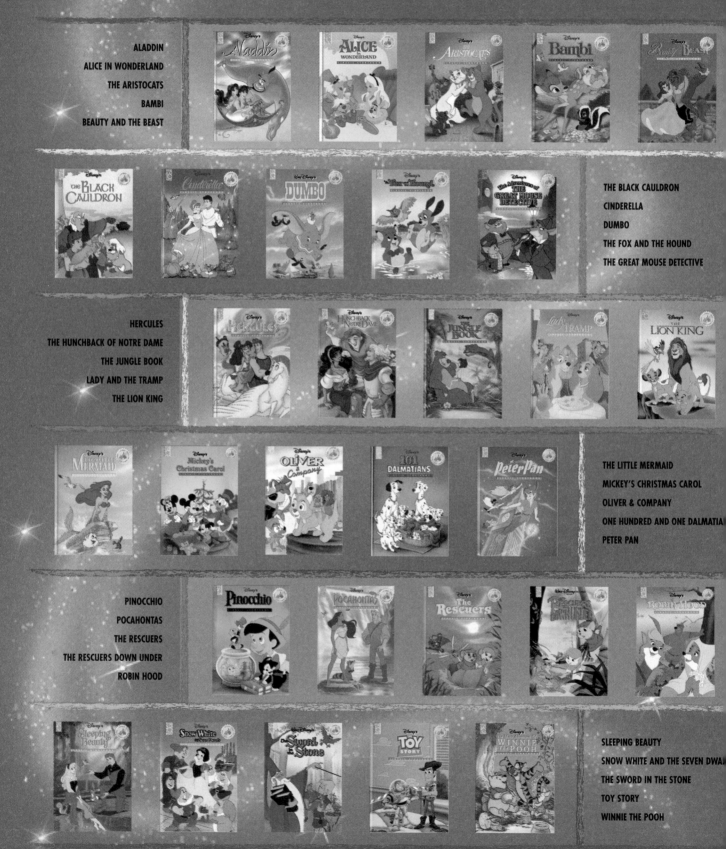

ALADDIN
ALICE IN WONDERLAND
THE ARISTOCATS
BAMBI
BEAUTY AND THE BEAST

THE BLACK CAULDRON
CINDERELLA
DUMBO
THE FOX AND THE HOUND
THE GREAT MOUSE DETECTIVE

HERCULES
THE HUNCHBACK OF NOTRE DAME
THE JUNGLE BOOK
LADY AND THE TRAMP
THE LION KING

THE LITTLE MERMAID
MICKEY'S CHRISTMAS CAROL
OLIVER & COMPANY
ONE HUNDRED AND ONE DALMATIANS
PETER PAN

PINOCCHIO
POCAHONTAS
THE RESCUERS
THE RESCUERS DOWN UNDER
ROBIN HOOD

SLEEPING BEAUTY
SNOW WHITE AND THE SEVEN DWARFS
THE SWORD IN THE STONE
TOY STORY
WINNIE THE POOH